Alexa
the Fashion Reporter Fairy

by Daisy Meadows

ORCHARD

www.rainbowmagic.co.uk

Jack Frost's Spell

I'm the king of designer fashion,
Looking stylish is my passion.
Ice Blue's the name of my fashion range,
Some people think my clothes are strange.

Do I care, though? Not a bit!
My designer label will be a hit.
The Fashion Fairies' magic will make that come true:
Soon everyone will wear Ice Blue!

Contents

Fashion Magic

"What shall we call our fashion magazine, Rachel?" Kirsty asked, tapping her pencil thoughtfully on her sketch pad. "I just can't think of a good title!"

The girls were in the beautiful landscaped park that surrounded the new *Tippington Fountains Shopping Centre*, an enormous building of chrome and glass. Kirsty had come to stay with Rachel for half-term, and Mrs Walker had taken them to the grand opening of *Tippington Fountains* earlier that week. Yesterday Rachel and Kirsty had attended a workshop for the Design-and-Make Competition at the shopping centre, and the girls had enjoyed it so much, they'd decided to create their own fashion magazine.

They were sitting on a picnic rug on a soft carpet of red, yellow and orange autumn 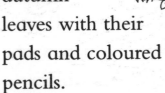 leaves with their pads and coloured pencils.

Rachel was finishing a design for
a T-shirt. "I'm not sure," she replied,
glancing up as more leaves drifted down
from the trees above them. "*Fashion for
Girls?*"

"How about *Fantastic Fashions?*"
suggested Rachel's dad. He was sitting
nearby on a park bench, reading a
newspaper.

"*Fabulous Fashions*?" Kirsty said, then shook her head. "No, that's not special enough. What about *Fashion Magic*?"

"Perfect!" Rachel said with a grin. She held up her sketch pad to show Kirsty her T-shirt design. The T-shirt was bright orange with "Tippington Fountains" written in gold and red letters across the front. Between the words Rachel had added a drawing of the spectacular fountains that were situated in the middle of the shopping centre. "I based the colours on the autumn leaves," Rachel added.

12

"I think that should be our front cover," Kirsty said, admiring the design. "And I want to interview you about the workshop we went to yesterday so that I can write an article for our magazine." Kirsty cleared her throat and held up a pretend microphone in front of Rachel. "So, Rachel," she said, "tell me what you did at the workshop yesterday."

"I wanted to make something really colourful, so I painted a rainbow on my jeans," Rachel explained.

"And how does it feel to be one of the competition

winners who'll be modelling in the charity fashion show at the end of this week?" asked Kirsty.

Rachel burst out laughing. "Well, you should know," she pointed out. "You were one of the competition winners as well! Your floaty scarf-dress was *gorgeous*."

"Girls," called Mr Walker from the bench. "You might be interested in this for your magazine." He handed over an insert that had been inside his newspaper.

Rachel and Kirsty stared at the glossy leaflet. The headline was "*Be cool as ice in these hot new designs from ICE BLUE!"* The clothes in the photos were all ice blue, and they looked rather strange. There was a jacket

with only one sleeve, and a pair of trousers with one short leg and one long. There was also a jumper knitted from blue plastic strips, and a pair of socks with holes instead of toes.

The girls exchanged horrified glances. They knew very well that Ice Blue was the fashion label created by none other than Jack Frost himself!

On the day the shopping centre opened, the girls had been thrilled when

their old friend Phoebe the Fashion
Fairy had invited them to Fairyland
for a fashion show. The show had been
organised by Phoebe's helpers, the seven
Fashion Fairies who looked after all
kinds of fashion in both the human and
fairy worlds. But the event had hardly
begun when Jack Frost and his goblins
gate-crashed the show, modelling their
own crazy blue outfits. Jack Frost had
announced that soon everyone, humans
and fairies alike, would be wearing his
Ice Blue clothes. And to help him achieve
his plan, Jack Frost and his goblins had
stolen the Fashion Fairies' magical
objects, and whisked them away to
Tippington Fountains.

"Jack Frost is determined to make
everyone wear his silly blue clothes!"

Rachel murmured to Kirsty. "I just hope we can stop him."

"We've managed to find *three* of the Fashion Fairies' magical objects so far," Kirsty reminded her. "Let's hope we find the others before the charity fashion show at the end of the week."

Rachel nodded and brushed aside a scarlet leaf that had landed on her sketch pad. There weren't many leaves on the trees now, Rachel thought, watching more float slowly to the ground. Soon it would be winter...

A flash of light above her head suddenly caught Rachel's attention.

Another leaf, sparkling in the autumn
sunshine, was drifting slowly down.
Leaves don't sparkle, Rachel thought, her
heart beating faster. But fairies do!

Quickly Rachel pointed out the
sparkling leaf to Kirsty.

"Oh!" Kirsty whispered. "Could it be–?"

Rachel put her finger to her lips and
pointed at her dad. Mr Walker was intent
on reading his newspaper and hadn't
noticed a thing, so the girls rushed across
the grass towards the falling leaf. They
cupped their hands together, and the
leaf landed lightly on their outstretched
palms. It wasn't a leaf at all – it was
a tiny, sparkly fairy. Her long shiny
blonde hair hung in a plait over one
shoulder, and she wore a blue dress with
a Peter Pan collar, knee-length socks and

chestnut-brown leather shoes. She also
had a matching leather shoulder bag.

"Hello, Alexa the Fashion Reporter
Fairy!" Rachel murmured softly.

Ice Blue is Cool!

"Girls, I must talk to you!" Alexa whispered, glancing at Mr Walker a little anxiously.

"Let's hide behind the tree," Kirsty suggested.

They all darted behind the tree out of sight, and Alexa breathed a sigh of relief.

"I'm thrilled to see you, girls," she
declared. "I need your help to get my
magic pen back from Jack Frost and his
naughty goblins!"

"Look at this, Alexa."
Rachel showed her
the Ice Blue leaflet.
"My dad found it in
his newspaper."

Alexa nodded sadly.
"Jack Frost is using the
magic of my special pen
to tell everyone about his crazy Ice Blue
outfits," she explained. "I need my pen so
that I can let everyone know about *all*
the different styles of fashion. Then they
can choose to wear what suits them. If
we don't find the pen soon, everyone will
only be wearing Ice Blue clothes!"

"Let's go and look for it," Kirsty suggested.

Alexa jumped into Rachel's pocket, and the girls hurried out from behind the tree.

"Dad, can we go into the shopping centre for a little while?" Rachel asked.

Her father looked up from his newspaper and nodded. "I'll meet you by the press office booth in about half an hour," he told them.

The girls headed to the shopping centre entrance. As

23

they approached the doors, they saw a woman on a bicycle pedalling furiously past them. She was red in the face and her long black hair was flying out behind her.

"She's in a hurry!" Rachel murmured.

The woman jumped off her bike, set it on its stand, and yanked her handbag out of the wicker shopping basket on the front of the bike. But the handbag fell open, tipping everything onto the ground.

"Oh, no!" the woman groaned.

Rachel and Kirsty stopped to help and began picking up her notebook, papers, pens, purse and mobile phone.

"Thank you so much," the woman said, taking her phone from Rachel. "I've had *such* an awful morning! My alarm didn't go off, and then I lost my notebook. By the time I found it, I was already really late, and then I had a flat tyre on my bike!" She sighed. "Thanks again, girls," she told them.

And, clutching
her handbag,
the woman
raced into
the shopping
centre.

"I wonder
who she is
and what she's
late for?" Kirsty
remarked as they
followed her inside.

Rachel didn't answer. She was staring
up at one of the large TV screens that
showed advertisements. On-screen,
models were posing in weird blue outfits
like the ones in the newspaper leaflet.

"Ice Blue again!" Rachel said.

The girls glanced around and were

dismayed when they realised that *all* the TV screens they could see were showing the same advertisement. Not only that, there were announcements every few minutes over the shopping centre's loudspeaker system.

"ICE BLUE!" a voice boomed out. "The ONLY clothes for people who love to look COOL!"

"Jack Frost's fashion label is
everywhere!" Kirsty pointed out, looking
worried. As the girls walked through the
crowded mall, they could see Ice Blue
clothes on
display in the
windows of
all the fashion
stores. There
were lots of
shoppers staring
admiringly at the clothes, too.

"Surely there must be some people who
don't like Ice Blue!" Kirsty said. "Maybe
we should try and interview shoppers for
our magazine. Can you see anyone you
know, Rachel?"

Rachel glanced around. "I think most
of Tippington is here!" she laughed. "Let's

search for Alexa's magic pen, and I'll
look for someone we can interview."

The girls walked on, keeping their
eyes open for the magical pen. Suddenly
Rachel gave an exclamation.

"There's Jodie Allen with her family,"
she said. "She's in my class at school."

Jodie was with her mum, her younger
brother, her teenage sister and her gran,
all of whom
Rachel knew.
They were
staring
into one of
the shop
windows
at a display
of Ice Blue
clothes.

The girls went over to them. "Hi, Jodie," Rachel said with a smile. "My friend Kirsty and I are making our own fashion magazine, and we wondered if we could interview you and your family about your favourite design labels?"

"Oh, that's easy, Rachel," Jodie said with a big grin. "We all love Ice Blue!"

"*All* of you?" Rachel repeated, shocked.

"Absolutely!" Mrs Allen agreed. "The clothes are really beautiful and unusual, and they suit everyone, whatever age you are."

"What about your other favourite labels?" asked Kirsty.

"We don't like any clothes now, except Ice Blue," Mrs Allen told her.

"My friends are all wearing Ice Blue, too," Jodie's sister chimed in. "It's really cool!"

"Even Jake loves Ice Blue," Jodie said, smiling at her little brother, "and he's not into clothes at all!"

"I'm thinking of buying that for myself." Jodie's gran

pointed at a blue coat in
the shop window.
The coat had
extra-long,
droopy sleeves,
a raggedy hem
and buttons stuck
all over it. "What
do you think?"

"Lovely!" the
rest of Jodie's family
chorused.

"Thanks for talking to us," Rachel said
politely as she and Kirsty moved away.

"They're all mad about Ice Blue!"
Kirsty murmured to her friend. "This is
terrible."

Alexa peeped out of Rachel's pocket.
"And it'll get worse unless we find my

pen!" she told them.

The girls walked on past various shops including *Pens'n' Paper Stationery, Hartley's Department Store* and *Fashion First.* Then ahead of them they spotted a crowd of people gathered around a giant TV screen, the biggest in the shopping centre.

"Oh, look!" Kirsty exclaimed, recognising the face that had just flashed up on the screen. "That's Ella McCauley!" The girls had met Ella, a well-known fashion designer, at the workshop the day before. Rachel and Kirsty had liked her very much, and they also loved the fun, casual clothes that she designed.

"Read an exclusive interview with Ella McCauley in the upcoming edition of

The Fountains Fashion News!" the voice-over said.

Alexa peeped out of Rachel's pocket. "At last!" she whispered with a grin. "Something that *isn't* about Ice Blue!"

The advertisement changed, and another face appeared on the screen.

It was a woman with long black hair whom Kirsty and Rachel recognised immediately.

"It's the woman on the bicycle!" Kirsty murmured.

"Welcome to *Fountains Fashion TV*," the woman said with a smile. "I'm your fashion reporter, Nicki Anderson, and today we're here live in the shopping centre to talk about the fashion label that's taking the world by storm – Ice Blue!"

The girls glanced at each other in dismay.

"And I have one of the Ice Blue models here with me right now," Nicki continued.

The camera moved off Nicki and onto the person standing next to her. Rachel and Kirsty could hardly believe their eyes when they saw a goblin smirking at the camera!

Nicki Needs Help

The goblin was wearing a patchwork jacket and trousers, made from squares of material in different shades of blue. The crowd of people watching the TV went crazy, cheering and clapping as the goblin paraded up and down.

"You look fabulous!" Nicki told the goblin. "Tell me, why are Ice Blue clothes so popular?"

"Because
everyone wants
to look as
handsome, cool
and fashionable
as I do," the goblin
replied. "And you
don't have to be green like me to look
good in Ice Blue clothes!"

The audience roared with laughter.

"And why *are* you green?" asked Nicki.

"It's face paint," the goblin explained
quickly. "Very on-trend!"

Rachel and Kirsty watched along with
everyone else as more goblins appeared
on-screen, modelling other outrageous
blue outfits. The watching crowd oohed
and aahed, and applauded loudly.

"I want one of those patchwork suits!"

Rachel heard a boy say to his friend.

"Me, too," his friend replied. "I *love* Ice Blue."

Meanwhile Kirsty was staring hard at the TV. "Look, Rachel," she murmured. The goblins were twirling around, showing off their outfits, and then scurrying off into the shop in the background behind Nicki Anderson. "I recognise that shop — it's *Pens'n' Paper.*"

"And that would be a *great* place to hide my magic pen!" Alexa whispered.

"Let's go!" said Rachel.

The girls scooted across the shopping centre, back to the *Pens'n' Paper* shop they'd passed earlier. They arrived, just in time to catch Nicki Anderson ending her live report.

"And that's all from me for the

moment," Nicki said to the camera. She was now wearing an Ice Blue baseball cap with a logo of Jack Frost. "Just remember – Ice Blue is the fashion label of the future!"

Nicki handed her microphone to the cameraman, and then she noticed the girls.

"Hello again," she said warmly. "Thanks for helping me this morning. Sorry I can't stay and chat, but I'm supposed to be interviewing Ella McCauley now for *The Fountains Fashion News*. Do you have the time?"

"Quarter past eleven," Rachel told her.

Nicki looked shocked. "Oh, no – I'm fifteen minutes late!" she exclaimed. "I was on my way to meet Ella, but I got cornered by the Ice Blue crew! Girls, could you help me carry my things to the press office booth? Maybe Ella is waiting for me there."

"Of course we will," said Rachel.

Nicki picked up her handbag and handed Kirsty her coat and Rachel her big notebook. Then the three of them ran through the crowds of shoppers to the press office booth.

"Is Ella McCauley anywhere

around?" Nicki asked the woman in the booth. "I'm late for an interview with her."

"Ella *was* here," the woman replied, "but she's gone outside into the park to be interviewed by another reporter."

"Oh, no!" Nicki sighed. "I hope Ella's got time to talk to me afterwards because I *really* need that interview! I'd better ring my editor and tell her what's happening."

"Shall we go outside and look for Ella?" asked Kirsty helpfully.

"Oh, would you?" Nicki said, taking out her phone. "That would be great!"

Rachel and Kirsty

hurried out of the shopping centre.

"Nicki's having lots of bad luck because my magic pen is missing!" Alexa said solemnly. "It's very kind of you to help her, girls."

"I hope Nicki doesn't get into trouble with her editor," Rachel remarked. She stopped and gazed around the huge gardens. "I wonder where Ella is."

"It would be easier to spot her if we could fly," Kirsty suggested.

"That's just what I was going to say!"

Alexa replied with a grin. They all
ducked behind a topiary hedge in the
shape of a swan. Then Alexa zoomed out
of Rachel's pocket and hovered above
the girls. With a sprinkle of magical fairy
dust from Alexa's wand,
Rachel and Kirsty
became fairy-
size.

The
three friends
whirled up
into the air
and began
to search the
gardens. They
flew over the tops
of the autumn trees and
the lake, but there was no sign of Ella.

After a while, though, Rachel spotted an ornate red and gold bandstand, half hidden among the trees.

"I can see Ella!" Rachel announced to Kirsty and Alexa. "She's sitting in the bandstand with the other reporter."

As they flew close, Rachel could see that Ella was showing her sketchbook and some fabric samples to the interviewer. But then Kirsty noticed the reporter himself. He was wearing an Ice Blue patchwork suit and enormous blue shoes.

"He's a goblin!" Kirsty realised. And clutched in the goblin's big green hand was Alexa's magic pen!

Furious Jack Frost

Quickly, Kirsty pointed out the goblin with the pen to Rachel and Alexa.

"We have to get it back!" Rachel said urgently as the three of them landed on the roof of the bandstand.

Alexa put her finger to her lips. "Let's listen to what the goblin's saying," she whispered. "We must think of a plan to grab my pen, but we'll have to wait until he's finished interviewing Ella."

"Your fashion designs are OK," the goblin was telling Ella, "but all these colours look  dreadful! The clothes would be much better if they were all in shades of blue."

"I like blue, but I prefer to use lots of different colours," Ella replied politely.

"Huh!" the goblin snorted in disgust. "That's nonsense! Blue is the best colour in the whole world! Why don't you join the Ice Blue team and work for us? After all, we're creating the fashion of the future!"

Rachel and Kirsty shook their heads at each other.

"Isn't he rude?" Rachel said in a low voice. "Ella's designs are beautiful *and* comfortable – not like Ice Blue!"

"Poor Ella," Kirsty sighed. "She's very polite, but she must be a bit fed up." Then her face lit up. "Oh – I have an idea!" Kirsty exclaimed. "But I need to be human-size again."

Swiftly the three of them flew down from the bandstand and fluttered behind a tree. A stream of glittery sparkles from Alexa's wand made Kirsty shoot up to her usual size.

Then she headed towards the bandstand.

"Sorry to interrupt," Kirsty called as she went up the steps. "But the shopping centre reporter, Nicki, is waiting for Ella at the press office booth."

The goblin glared at Kirsty, but Ella jumped to her feet immediately. Kirsty could see that she looked very relieved.

"Thank you, Kirsty," Ella said. She smiled at the goblin. "And thank you for interviewing me."

The goblin didn't smile back. "You can't go yet!" he protested sulkily. But Ella had already hurried down the steps.

Instantly Rachel and Alexa swooped into the bandstand. The goblin saw them and gave a screech of rage.

"Pesky fairies!" he hollered. He raced for the steps to escape, but Kirsty blocked his path.

"We'd like Alexa's magic pen back, please," Kirsty said firmly.

"Never!" the goblin shrieked. Rachel and Alexa fluttered around his head, attempting to distract him, and the goblin hit out at them frantically.

Meanwhile Kirsty tried to grab the pen, but the goblin kept spinning out of her reach.

"HEY!" An angry shout made them all stop and look around. To Kirsty's horror, she saw Jack Frost striding across the gardens towards them. He was wearing his Ice Blue suit, and, like Ella, he carried a portfolio and a book of fabric samples.

"It's Jack Frost!" Kirsty gasped to Rachel and Alexa. "Quick – hide!"

Rachel and Alexa whizzed back up to the top of the bandstand out of sight. The goblin burst out laughing.

"Not so brave now, are you?" he jeered, still clutching Alexa's pen tightly.

Jack Frost stomped up the bandstand steps. He looked very angry indeed. But Kirsty was surprised to see that Jack Frost wasn't glaring at *her* – instead he was staring furiously at the goblin.

"What are you doing?" he roared.

The goblin jumped with fright. "Um –
er – I was just interviewing –" he began.

"Why are you using the magic pen to
interview this silly designer?" Jack Frost
demanded, pointing
at Kirsty. "You're
supposed to be
interviewing *me*
about Ice Blue!"
He turned to
Kirsty. "Time
you were
going!" he
snapped.

Kirsty hurried
down the steps and popped behind a
nearby tree where she could see and hear
everything that was going on. Rachel
and Alexa rushed to join her.

"If you can't do the job right, I'll do it myself!" Jack Frost told the goblin. He pointed his wand at the goblin and unleashed a bolt of icy magic. Alexa's pen flew out of the goblin's hand and into Jack Frost's jacket pocket.

Kirsty, Rachel and Alexa glanced at each other in silent horror. How on earth were they going to get the pen back *now*?

Who's Got a Pen?

Impatiently Jack Frost waved the goblin away, and he trudged off, kicking gloomily at the piles of autumn leaves. Meanwhile, Jack Frost sat down on the bandstand steps. He took out the pen and an ice-blue notebook, and cleared his throat.

"So Mr Frost, you're clearly a very talented fellow!" Jack Frost said admiringly in a deep voice. "May we see your wonderful portfolio and fabric samples?" Then he slid across to the opposite side of the step. "Of course you can," Jack Frost said in his normal voice. And, smiling icily, he opened his portfolio. "As you can see, all my designs have the Jack Frost silhouette logo."

"Jack Frost is interviewing himself!" Kirsty whispered. She, Rachel and Alexa tried not to laugh.

"These are truly remarkable designs, Mr Frost," Jack Frost went on, swapping seats again. "May I ask what is your  inspiration for Ice Blue?"

He slid back across the step.

"Well, *me*, really," Jack Frost replied with a smug grin. "I'm so handsome, I inspire myself!"

"Jack Frost has just give me an idea," Rachel murmured. "I think I know how we can get the pen back! Alexa, will you make me human-size again?"

"Of course," Alexa agreed.

"But I have to be dressed in Ice Blue clothes!" Rachel told her.

Kirsty watched as a burst of Alexa's fairy magic restored Rachel to her normal size. But now she was wearing a crazy Ice Blue outfit – trousers made of diamond-shaped blue patches, and an enormous baggy T-shirt with the Jack Frost logo on it.

Kirsty couldn't help laughing.

Rachel grinned at her. "It's your turn, Kirsty!" she declared.

Alexa waved her wand. Now Kirsty was also dressed from head to toe in a weird blue outfit – a back-to-front jacket, clown trousers and a baseball cap with an enormous peak. This time it was Rachel's turn to burst out laughing. Then she quickly whispered her plan to Alexa and Kirsty. They nodded, and Alexa flew to hide under the peak of Kirsty's cap.

Quickly the girls hurried out from behind the tree.

"Look!" Rachel yelled, sounding breathless with excitement. "There's the famous designer who makes all these gorgeous Ice Blue clothes!"

Jack Frost heard and stared at them.

"Oh, yes!" said Kirsty. "Let's go and say hello and tell him how much we *love* his fabulous outfits!"

The girls rushed over to the bandstand. Jack Frost jumped to his feet and greeted them with a gracious smile. "I can see you're fans of my designer label," he said, looking thrilled.

"You've got great taste and style!"

"We've thrown all our other clothes away," Rachel told him.

"We're only going to wear Ice Blue from now on!" added Kirsty.

Jack Frost nodded. "Soon *everyone* in the whole world will be wearing Ice Blue," he replied proudly. "I'm doing an interview to spread the word about my designs."

Rachel and Kirsty glanced around the bandstand.

"But where's the reporter?" Kirsty asked.

"I'm interviewing *myself*," Jack Frost explained. He sighed. "But it's not easy."

"Maybe *we* could interview you?" Rachel suggested. "It would be such an honour!"

"We promise we'll tell *everyone* how great Ice Blue is," said Kirsty.

"That's a good idea," Jack Frost replied with a smug smile. "But I'll only do the interview if I can tell you what questions to ask."

"OK," Rachel agreed. She turned to Kirsty. "Do you have a pen?" Rachel asked her.

Kirsty shook her head. "Sorry."

"I don't have one either." Rachel frowned. She looked at Jack Frost. "Could we borrow *your* pen?"

Jack Frost hesitated. Rachel waited for his answer, hoping she didn't look too nervous. Would her plan work?

Girls in the Spotlight

Jack Frost scowled.

"Well..." he muttered reluctantly, "I suppose so. But I want it back as soon as you've finished the interview."

He handed the pen over to Rachel, who sighed with relief. At that moment Alexa swooped out from under Kirsty's baseball cap and zoomed over to Rachel.

Jack Frost gave a shout of rage, but it all happened too fast for him to do anything. The instant Alexa touched the pen, it shrank to its Fairyland size, and she tucked it safely away inside her shoulder bag.

"You think you're so clever!" Jack Frost sneered, stamping his foot. "But you won't stop me! I still have three of the Fashion Fairies' magical objects left, and soon my Ice Blue clothes will take over the world!" And he flounced off in a temper.

"Girls, I can't thank

you enough." Alexa
beamed at Rachel and
Kirsty. "And to show
you just how grateful
I am, let me change

your terrible clothes!" She pointed her
wand at Rachel and Kirsty and in an
instant, the two girls were back in the
clothes they'd been wearing earlier.

"Thanks, Alexa," Kirsty said with a
grin. "I could hardly see where I was
going in that enormous baseball cap!"

"I must rush back to Fairyland and
share the good news with everyone,"
Alexa said happily. "Now fashion
reporters everywhere will be able to tell
people about *all* the wonderful clothes
they can buy, not just Ice Blue. Goodbye,
girls – and I'd love to see your fashion

magazine when it's finished!" Then Alexa
vanished in a mist of sparkling fairy dust.

"That was close!" Kirsty sighed as
she and Rachel hurried back into the
shopping centre. "I didn't think Jack Frost
was going to let us borrow Alexa's pen!"

"Me neither," Rachel agreed. "We'd
better go straight to the press office booth.
It's time to meet my dad."

"I wonder if Nicki
did her interview
with Ella after all?"
Kirsty said.

When the girls
reached the press
office booth, they
saw that Nicki
was in the middle
of interviewing Ella.

They were surrounded by a crowd of people. Mr Walker was at the front, so Rachel and Kirsty went to join him.

"And what do you think about this new Ice Blue label?" Nicki was asking Ella.

"Well, the designer has some very unusual ideas," Ella replied carefully, "but the colour blue doesn't suit *everyone*, and

I always think
it's best to let
people choose
what they
want to wear

depending on what suits them."

Nicki nodded. "And can you tell
us about the Design-and-Make
Competition you were involved in
yesterday?" she said.

"We were looking for wonderful outfits
for the charity fashion show at the end
of this week," Ella explained. "We wanted
original designs with imagination and
flair." Just then she spotted Rachel and
Kirsty at the front of the crowd. "Would
you like to interview two of the winners,
Nicki?" And Ella beckoned the girls
forward.

The audience applauded as Rachel and Kirsty joined Nicki and Ella. Mr Walker proudly looked on.

"So, girls, how does it feel to be competition winners?" Nicki asked with a smile.

"Great!" said Kirsty, feeling a little shy.

"Fantastic!" Rachel added.

"Tell us about your designs," Nicki went on.

Rachel briefly described her rainbow

jeans and Kirsty talked about her scarf-dress. Nicki and the audience all looked very interested.

"Thank you, girls," Nicki told them. "And we'll look forward to seeing you modelling your outfits at the charity fashion show later this week!"

As the audience applauded, Rachel and Kirsty smiled at each other. They were both thrilled that they'd already found four of the Fashion Fairies' magical objects.

But the girls knew that the charity
fashion show would be a disaster, and
everything to do with fashion in the
human and fairy worlds would be ruined,
unless they found the last three objects
and returned them safely to the Fashion
Fairies. They still had some exciting
adventures to come!

**Now it's time for Kirsty and
Rachel to help...**

Matilda the Hair stylist Fairy

Read on for a sneak peek...

Kirsty Tate and her best friend Rachel
Walker gazed into the salon mirrors in
excitement. They were sitting side by side,
waiting to have their hair styled in the
coolest salon in town – *Snip & Clip*.

"What's it going to be, girls?" asked
Blair, the head hair stylist.

"I just want the ends trimmed off my
hair," said Kirsty.

"What about you, Rachel?" asked
Claire, the other stylist. "Are you going to
try something more daring?"

Rachel's eyes sparkled as she looked at
Claire in the mirror.

"I'd really love to have lots of tiny braids all over my head," she said. "Could you do that?"

"There's nothing that Claire can't do with hair!" said Blair with a laugh. "Let's get started."

The girls looked down at the trolley that stood between them. It was full of special hairdressing scissors, combs and brushes, and pretty hair clips, bands and jewels. They looked up and smiled at each other.

"I love getting my hair done," said Rachel. "It's even more fun when you're here with me!"

Kirsty was spending the autumn half-term in Tippington with Rachel. As a special treat, Mrs Walker had brought them to the new salon in the *Tippington Fountains Shopping Centre*. Mrs Walker was reading a magazine in the waiting area. She was planning to have her hair styled for a party that she and Mr Walker were going to that night.

"*Tippington Fountains* is the best shopping centre ever," said Kirsty. "We're so lucky – we've visited every single day since it opened!"

Read Matilda the Hair Stylist Fairy to find out what adventures are in store for Kirsty and Rachel!

Meet the
Fashion Fairies

If Kirsty and Rachel don't find the Fashion Fairies'
magical objects, Jack Frost will ruin fashion forever!

www.rainbowmagicbooks.co.uk

Meet the fairies, play games
and get sneak peeks at
the latest books!

www.rainbowmagicbooks.co.uk

There's fairy fun for everyone on
our wonderful website.
You'll find great activities, competitions, stories and
fairy profiles, and also a special newsletter.

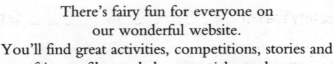

Competition!

Here's a friend who Kirsty and Rachel met in an earlier story. Use the clues below to help you guess her name. When you have enjoyed all seven of the Fashion Fairies books, arrange the first letters of each mystery fairy's name to make a special word, then send us the answer!

CLUES

1. This fairy loves wearing the colour purple.

2. She is one of the Weather Fairies.

3. This fairy wears a necklace in the shape of a raindrop.

The fairy's name is _ _ _ _ _ _   the   _ _ _ _   Fairy

We will put all of the correct entries into a draw and select one winner to receive a special Fashion Fairies goody bag. Your name will also be featured in a forthcoming Rainbow Magic story!

Enter online now at www.rainbowmagicbooks.co.uk

The Complete
Book of Fairies

Packed with secret fairy facts
and extra-special rainbow reveals, this magical guide
includes all you need to know about your favourite
Rainbow Magic friends.

Out Now!